God Believes in You

Holly Bea
Illustrated by Kim Howard

H J Kramer
Starseed Press
Tiburon, California

Art director: Linda Kramer
Design and production: Jan Phillips, San Anselmo, California

Library of Congress Cataloging-in-Publication Data

Bea, Holly, 1956–
God believes in you / Holly Bea ; illustrated by Kim Howard.
p. cm.
Summary: When Holly's bull mastiff, Buddy, is afraid, embarrassed, or
worried, he feels better when he remembers God is watching over him.
ISBN 1-932073-08-6 (Hard Cover : alk. paper)
[1. God—Fiction. 2. Dogs—Fiction. 3. Bullmastiff—Fiction. 4. Stories
in rhyme.] I. Howard, Kim, ill. II. Title.
PZ8.3.B3485Go 2004
[E]—dc22

                                        2003024073

H J Kramer / Starseed Press
P.O. Box 1082, Tiburon, California 94920

Printed in China
10 9 8 7 6 5 4 3 2

For Milli Baranowski, who taught me
the art of being an aunt.
H.B.

To Gretchen Sackett, the most generous,
loving, and supportive godmother to
my daughter, and loyal friend to me.
K.H.

When you have a task to do,
But don't think you can follow through,
Let go of fear and know it's true,
That God believes in you.

If one you love has gone away,
Forever or for just a day,
You're not alone, don't be afraid,
'Cause God is there for you.

If you run into someone mean,
And they should bruise your self-esteem,
It doesn't really mean a thing,
When God believes in you.

When you don't know what choice to make,
Or which path is the best to take,
Just breathe in deep and take a break,
Let God believe in you.

If life is getting kind of rough,
And you aren't feeling very tough,
When you don't think you're good enough,
Let God believe in you.

If you think you failed the test,
And you can't keep up with the rest,
Someone knows that you're the best,
'Cause God believes in you.

If you forget the golden rule,
Or misbehave while you're at school,
Apologize and know it's true,
God still believes in you.

When life is feeling quite unfair,
And it seems more than you can bear,
Remember someone's always there,
'Cause God believes in you.

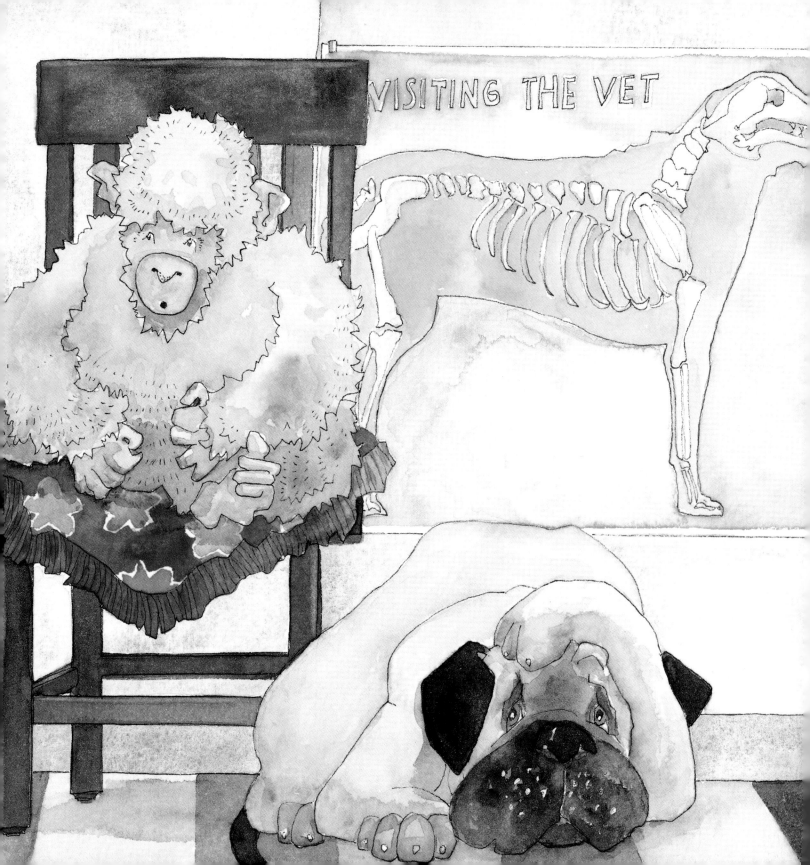

If sometimes you don't have a clue,
And wonder just what you should do,
Your inner voice is always true,
'Cause God believes in you.

If someone really needs a friend,
If there are fences you can mend,
You'll find the blessings in the end,
When God believes in you.

If you can give a friend advice,
Or help a neighbor once or twice,
It's really not a sacrifice,
When God believes in you.

If you are tempted to do wrong,
Or go somewhere you don't belong,
Walk away, don't go along,
Let God believe in you.

When you've created quite a mess,
And you are feeling in distress,
It doesn't make you any less,
Since God believes in you.

If you're reaching for the stars,
And just can't seem to stretch that far,
It doesn't matter where you are,
God still believes in you.

So don't forget to do your part,
Do your best to make your mark,
Believe in God with all your heart,
'Cause God believes in you.